I am
Edmund

I am
Edmund

Alexandra Glynn

RESOURCE *Publications* • Eugene, Oregon

I AM EDMUND

Wipf & Stock
An Imprint of Wipf and Stock Publishers
199 W. 8th Ave., Suite 3
Eugene, OR 97401

www.wipfandstock.com

PAPERBACK ISBN: 978-1-4982-3542-6
HARDCOVER ISBN: 978-1-4982-3544-0

Manufactured in the U.S.A.

Contents

Chapter One

———◦———

"Depart from me, O Lord, for I am a sinful man," I said. "Amen." The congregation began to sing a hymn. I moved from behind the pulpit to the central path between the pews, found an empty seat towards the back in the middle of a bench, and sat down. The trembling in my hands slowly subsided as I held the songbook and sang along with the congregation.

Through the window to my right I could see the trees just beginning to bud leaves on the trees right outside the building. I remembered my garden for a brief second and pondered if I should weed it tomorrow after work. Then the organist pulled out more stops for the last verse and I was pulled back into the music and the sermon of the words in the hymn. When the hymn ended a mother of five children who sat near me leaned over and greeted me. "Can I speak with you?" she asked. She had brown hair and was wearing a brown suit. She dug into a yellow and orange plaid diaper bag next to her and gave a pacifier to the one-year-old she held on her lap.

"Sure." It seemed this was to be my first counseling session in this congregation. I said a quick prayer for help as I straightened my suit coat.

The woman hesitated, bouncing her one-year-old on her lap. "Even though you're our brand new minister and we all want to be welcoming, I have a difficulty I'd like discuss with you." She laughed nervously and tried to pry her necklace away from the child in her arms. "But I don't want to scare you away when you just got here—it's my sister, my older sister. She lost faith and she comes to me with so many questions. I want to help her and encourage her to freely ask questions. But I can't get her to agree to come to services and get answers in the congregation and from the preached Word of God." The woman moved over to the edge of the pew, stood up, and began pushing the stroller in the aisle. I moved over too. In the woman's stroller there was a three-year-old asleep. We watched him sleeping for a moment. Then I got up too and went to stand by the wall in front of her, leaning on it, waiting for her to continue. Finally she said, "She agreed to talk with you. I told her we're getting a new young minister from a small town." She smoothed her brown hair back with one hand and patted her baby's head with the other. "I mean, everyone has been talking about it for weeks." I took the stroller handle from her and began to push the stroller back and forth. She looked at me hopefully, "Will you visit her?"

"Of course." I fished out a notebook and pen from my inside suit coat pocket. "What kinds of questions does she ask?"

"Oh, ever so many. She asks about gossiping, drinking wine, abuse, sports. She has a friend who is in some church Bible group and so her friend gets her asking all kinds of questions about the Bible." The woman paused and we waited for a crowd of teenagers to go by the narrow aisle between us. I nodded and smiled at them though they were all unfamiliar to me. The mother I was speaking with knew almost all of them, and greeted them all. After they had all gone by she said, "Oh, sorry, I suppose I should have introduced you."

"That's okay." I watched the teenagers filing out of the church. I had a few relatives in the congregation and one of the teens had looked familiar so maybe I knew one of them. I would be getting to know them all well in the coming weeks, I thought, because I planned to visit the homes of each family in the congregation as soon as I could. I turned back to the mother, "Is there anything from the Bible that you can tell me to look at beforehand?"

"Yes, she says the Bible is full of passages that are anti-woman."

"Ah," I said. In my mind I went through my bookshelves at home. I had gotten quite a few books on different religious topics from an ordained pastor friend of mine who had given them to me when I became a speaker of the Word. Some were about women. But I had not read almost any of them.

"You are Heidi, right?" I asked the woman.

"Yes."

"Heidi, I'll be glad to visit your sister. What is her name?"

"Amy."

"She has perhaps been reading feminist interpretations of the Bible."

"It seems like it. What should I tell her? I mean, she said she would visit you, but she has backed out of these things before."

"Tell her to read the Bible itself, rather than commentary on it written by those who write without the Spirit. And look in Corinthians where it says that the matters of faith are to be spiritually discerned. For example, I might not be given to understand why at the end of Judges a concubine is hurt. But I do know there is a spiritual lesson in that text, and that it is only discerned by the Spirit. But woe to me if I ascribe evil to God. God never advises or authorizes evil in his Word, so if we don't understand a text, we tip our hat, give glory to God, praying in the Spirit."

The mother dug in her diaper bag. "Ok. Let me write that text down. What did you say?"

I got out a pen and wrote it on one of the pages of my little notebook and gave it to her. Sometimes I wrote messages to myself on my smartphone instead, but usually I forgot about it and went with pen and paper. I wrote the text, plus my phone number and gave her the slip of paper. "How old is your sister?" I asked her.

"Thirty-two. I'm thirty-three. My husband's name is Erik. You and I are the same age, actually." I remembered being told that someone had done a brief bio of me and printed it in the church bulletin.

"Everyone knows me already then, but I don't know many people here. Introduce me to your children." Heidi did and we chatted about children and growing older for a few minutes. We made plans to try to meet at a coffee shop while the kids were in school next Wednesday. Heidi said she would text me one way or the other.

Heidi's one-year-old had settled down and Heidi said, "Here I am monopolizing you. Everyone's looking our way, wanting to get to know you." She began to walk me down the aisle towards the back of the church to the people standing around visiting there. She introduced me to so many people that I finally took my notebook back out and started taking names. Sometimes I took phone numbers too if I got invites. I ended up with almost a half dozen invitations. When there were only a few people left in the back of the church, one of the elderly women I had just met, whose name was Janet, asked me curiously if I was always going to stay until the last person left. I told her I probably would, because I wouldn't want to miss a minute of visiting. Since she seemed knowledgeable about all the people, the customs, and how things were normally done, I asked her if she would accept visitors on Tuesday. She welcomed me, and as she gave me directions to her place, I helped the usher turn out the lights and lock the door.

Just outside the church door someone had planted two large pots with spring flowers. I checked the soil on them and lifted up the leaves, looking for weeds. The soil felt moist and the flowers bloomed with health.

Janet laughed as she watched me. "You like gardening and flowers, I heard," she said.

"Just a hobby. Someone has been doing a good job with these."

Janet and I greeted and parted. As I walked through the parking lot I reflected that the flood of invitations was probably not going to last, but I was determined to enjoy the moment while it was here.

I waved goodbye to Janet and got into my car. I drove the seven minutes to my house, changed out of my suit, cleaned up a bit, repotted a couple flowers, watered my tomatoes, and then got back into my car to drive to what was going to be my first Sunday afternoon dinner visit.

Chapter Two

———◦———

*T*HE BONN FAMILY HAD invited me to Sunday dinner. They live in the suburb I live in. Their place is about ten miles from my place. It's a beige brick house trimmed in white. It was easy for me to find—I parked on a driveway with about eight other cars crammed in it. I walked by a small flower garden in the front yard and saw some tall sunflowers peeking around the corners of the wide porch as I went up the front steps. Carefully stationed bikes leaned on a side garage surrounded by a neat lawn.

I petted the dog on the porch and rang the doorbell. An awkward teenager greeted me. I learned from him that he was the Bonns' youngest child. They had eleven children, six boys and five girls. Five of the Boon children were not married: The boy who met me at the door, a man around thirty years old, and three daughters in their late twenties and early thirties. As the youngest in the family led me through the entryway to the big room that had a kitchen to one side, a dining area in the middle, and a sitting area on the other side, I saw that dinner was being served. So I sat right down and greeted everyone. Mr. and Mrs. Bonn, who had known my parents many years ago, introduced me to their unmarried children and one of the married sons who was there with his wife and children.

The youngest of the Bonn girls, Maddie, sat across from me. She had short very blond hair, clear blue eyes, and a wide smile. She had on a bright red dress, the color of some of the richest red flowers outside the church. As she passed me the potatoes she asked me somewhat challengingly, "So why did Elijah slaughter all the prophets of Baal in 1 Kings 18?" Then she picked up her fork and began to eat, watching me and ignoring her father's lifted eyebrows.

I was glad I had just spent the evening a few nights ago reading the prophets because I was able to answer her simply, "As I understand it, the text teaches about false teachings. Elijah shows that those who taught such things as the prophets of Baal taught, were teaching the teachings of death and condemnation. God sent Elijah his prophet to make this manifest to all the people as it says in Hosea 6 and in 2 Kings 17 and in the very last chapter of 2nd Chronicles. It is a matter of life and death. Also, Paul writes about this text in Romans 11, saying that it is a text teaching about how God chooses and keeps a grace kingdom of children here on this earth."

Mr. Bonn, the father, whose name was James, had looked chagrined at his daughter's question but now he smiled and me and said in a jolly way to his children around the table, "Well, there you have it. Are there any other Bible questions for the new speaker of the Word?"

"Dad, don't tease him," Freddie, the thirty-year-old unmarried son said.

"I'm very serious," Mr. Bonn said. "We seldom enough discuss the Scriptures around our table and in the living room. We'll have to have you over often," he said to me, his eyes twinkling.

"Yes," Freddie said drily, "The girls can spend the afternoon asking the minister Bible questions."

"Now who is teasing?" Maddie responded, blushing a little.

I tried to be gallant about the teasing and turned to talk with the children who were seated next to me. Inwardly I groaned and hoped I wasn't going to have to experience marriage teasing much. I had just moved from a very small congregation of mostly elderly people in the locality of the school I had been attending, and the elderly people had teased me somewhat, but fortunately there had not been a large number of single women to get teased about. I knew the teasing was good natured and done in fun though, and I also knew, because my mother had told me, that this new congregation would have many single people in it.

"What about chapter 36 of Genesis? Why are all those lists and genealogies in the Bible?" The question was from one of the older Bonn girls, Michelle, who they called Shelly. She had long blondish hair and wore a chunky necklace with what looked like rune inscriptions on it.

"That's right before the Joseph story starts, right?" I stalled.

"Yes." She waited for elaboration.

"And the chapter contains lists about Esau. We can see from the Joseph story that Joseph's brothers had fallen from faith. But we see them struggling with bitterness, a demanding spirit, and fornication, way back in chapter 34. The chapters in between are there at least in part to describe the growth of the kingdom of Esau at that time, and the spread of its virulent teachings."

Shelly considered this, then said, "Hold on a minute." Her greenish blue eyes considered me. "How do you get that from the 34th chapter of Genesis?"

"By what the brothers say at the very end of the chapter." I was getting a little worried that the conversation was getting into such a deep topic, but Mr. Bonn and Mrs. Bonn were attentively listening, as were their children. Even the grandchildren were peacefully eating slices of homemade bread slopped in the rich roast gravy.

Freddy's brow was furrowed as I glanced at him. "And what exactly was that?" he asked.

I took another piece of bread and spread butter over it. "This is good bread," I said to Mrs. Bonn.

"I didn't make it," she said. "Lara made it." Lara was the other single sister, darker haired and shy. I gave her as friendly a smile as I could muster and thanked her for the bread.

I turned to Freddie. "Their own words testify against them. Simon and Levi have women divided into two categories. They think that some women are to be treated badly, and some are to be treated with decency and respect. But consider chapter four of John. Jesus says that all women, no matter who they are or what their past is, are to be treated with respect and dignity. The brothers have fallen deeply into error in this matter. Perhaps this is one of the sins Joseph rebuked them about in chapter 37."

"I'm completely confused," Freddie said. "What did Simon and Levi say?"

"They said, 'Shall he deal with our sister as with whore?'" I said.

"Oh. I guess that is a revealing statement."

Freddie chewed his bread, thinking about what I had said. Then he said, "It's a good lesson. I myself have struggled with the different kinds of teachings on this topic."

"Well, it is a serious enough topic, that is for sure," Mr. Bonn said. Then he turned to me, "You know, young man, you should tell us more about yourself. I feel we get to know our ministers through their sermons, but now that we have you here, we can hear you tell us about yourself informally too."

"I am Edmund," I said, a little embarrassed. "I work as a manager at a big chain superstore. I'm almost thirty-three, not very tall, brown-haired and brown-eyed and I have been a speaker of the Word for a little over two years now."

"Tell us about your family," Maddie prompted. She had been getting the coffee ready and now brought it to the table and began pouring everyone a cup.

"I am an only child. My mother lives about three hours away in a nursing home, and my dad passed away about ten years ago. My parents were married late in life."

"Is that what you're going to do? Get married late in life?" Freddie's question was playful. I looked over at Shelly. I could tell she was pondering what we had been discussing. But what were her thoughts?

I gave Freddie a quick half-grin. "You never know. Whatever is meant. But I have some questions now for you about the area." I began to ask them about what problems I might encounter. Mr. Bonn told me that from his perspective there seemed to be problems that were as old as Adam, teenager troubles, marriage difficulties, bullying, overzealous watchfulness of others, gossiping, love of the world, and the like. We adults moved to the sitting area with our coffee and I asked Mr. Bonn if he thought that people would be coming to me desiring to visit or if I would be better off reaching out first. Mr. Bonn thought a while, then he told me of a few families and individuals who he thought might really need a visitor, but might not be bold enough to ask. I got out my little notebook and wrote down the names. They were shut-ins and parents with children who had lost faith, for the most part. I thanked Mr. Bonn and we discussed the Bible more. He seemed genuinely curious about some very obscure passages and it was all I could do to keep up with him. And here at first I had thought he was unhappy with Maddie's bringing up Bible texts for discussion! He and I went through a few cups of coffee between us. Freddie and Shelly listened in and offered a few comments here and there but Mr. Bonn was the one who kept me on my toes. I vowed to read the Bible more, thinking, now this is good for me to be put to these questions and to be forced to think so much about the Word of God. For some reason, God is allowing this to be how my afternoon is going.

Finally Mr. Bonn laughed and looked at the clock, surprised as I was to see how late it had gotten. Freddie, Maddie, Shelly and I went outside and played volleyball for an hour. They had a net set up out back. A few more single people came over and we played with a bigger group. Then someone built a bonfire and we sat around it singing songs until late into the night. When almost everyone had left I sat on a log staring into the flames. Shelly came and sat next to me, watching the sparks fly upward. I threw twigs onto the fire and observed how they caught flame. Shelly handed me a cup of coffee. What was this, my sixth cup? I took it anyway. "Did you have a good day?" she asked me.

"I did," I said. "You are very blessed in your family."

"I am," she said as we watched the orange and red colors of the fire playing in the darkness. It was early in the year so there were only a few bugs. Freddie was sawing logs on a tree over on the edge of the clearing in which the bonfire had been built. Shelly said, "I want to ask you about something serious." Then she told me about her sister Maddie, who had just broken an engagement with a young man. I asked her what I might do to help and she said to just be extra patient with Maddie. She said she herself tried to go out of her way to include Maddie.

"Like tonight," she said. "Maddie stayed the whole time and visited. She didn't seem depressed at all."

"That's good," I said.

"She's better than she was when I got home from Germany," Shelly went on, looking at the fire sparks flying upwards.

"You were in Germany?"

"Yes, to study."

"Really?"

"Yes, Luther's Bible, for example."

"That's neat." I looked at the firelight making her hair shine and waited for her to go on.

"Did you know in Romans where it says, 'He is the propitiation for our sins,' in Luther's translation it says, 'He is the mercy-seat for our sins.'"

"Oh, that's better," I said. "'Propitiation' is a hard word."

"Yes, but do people all know what the mercy-seat is?" she asked.

I contemplated her. "I guess I never thought it could be possible not to know what the mercy-seat is, the throne of grace."

"Yes, that's true, we sing about it so often."

Then we began talking about how easy it was to get down or depressed and how we need to help each other out. The fire died down and we were still talking. Through Shelly that night I learned about most of the people around our age. I asked many questions and wrote down names to help me remember. Shelly had lived here her whole life and she was a nurse at the local clinic so she saw many people every day in her job. I asked her about those who weren't in faith—were there any that she thought might need me to reach out to them. She couldn't think of anyone specific; she only encouraged me to freely invite people to services whenever the chance came.

When the fire was almost completely gone out I got up and stretched. Only Freddie was left outside; he was cleaning up the fire pit area. We greeted each other goodnight and I apologized for staying so late. "I know myself well enough to know that it is going to happen again," I told him.

"You're welcome any time," he responded.

That's how God made me, I thought, as I got into my car and drove home. And now I had a huge congregation and a whole new neighborhood, plus people at my work place and other places in the community. I would meet them all, I vowed. I thought of Paul's words, "I have become all things to all people that I might win some."

Chapter Three

*T*HE NEXT DAY, MONDAY, when I got home from work I began planting another garden out back. The one I had planted the day I first moved in seemed too small after I weeded it. It was a little late in the season to start another garden but I cleared a spot and hoed it out so I would have it ready for the next year. I stood surveying my work, trying to decide what to do with the fresh empty soil in front of me. Then, my hands all stained with dirt, I pulled my notebook out of my shirt pocket. Who to call? I debated texting Shelly to ask if there was a bonfire somewhere. Tomorrow I was going to Janet's but tonight maybe there were some elders who would enjoy a visitor. My eyes fell on the name Czernak. It was on the bottom of the first page of my list. I wondered if Heidi had mentioned them or if it had been Mr. Bonn. Who were they, though? I went inside and looked them up by name, number, and city. I called the number. A child answered.

"Are your folks home?"

"Sure, here's my mom."

I could hear a woman shouting at someone about some cats. Then her voice came on the phone, short of breath and suspicious, "Hello, who is this?"

"Hi. I am Edmund, a new pastor in town. I was hoping to get to know people in the area and wondered if you would mind if I came to visit. I have your address and I notice you live just five minutes from me."

"You can come over and help me do the dishes and clean up," the woman said coldly.

"Okay. Sounds fun. I'll need overalls and my work boots." My answer disconcerted her and her disposition toward me improved a little. I told her I would be there in an hour. I puttered around the house, read a little, called my mom and cleaned up my garden clothes. By five minutes to seven I was in my car and on my way to the Czernak home.

A woman I presumed was Mrs. Czernak was weeding in a garden next to a big white one-story house with a broad front lawn. There were about five cars and pick-ups parked out behind the garage, but other than that the yard was free of clutter. I got out of my car and went towards the rows carefully marked out with cucumbers, carrots, radishes, beans, watermelon, and strawberries. There were three big rows of raspberry bushes behind the garden and to one side of them were about six rows of corn. Mrs. Czernak put down her trowel when she saw me, came and greeted me, and then went in to get me a cup of coffee after seating me on her porch.

When she came back out she had three children following her. She introduced them as Lacy, Mary Ellen, and Sam. I asked her why she needed help cleaning but she didn't answer straight out. She only told me that things had been chaotic lately for her. We sat and chatted, smelling the fresh greenery all around us. "It looks wonderful," I said.

"What?"

"The garden."

"Oh."

She offered to give me a tour of it. We walked down a little stone path to the vegetables. Behold the big stands of strawberries and raspberries I saw she had rhubarb. She got down and pulled a few stray weeds. I wanted to help her, but I had offered to clean, so I watched until she got up and went into the house. I followed her back inside. "Why don't I start on the dishes, and then do the living area," I said, doing a quick survey of the rooms that I could see. Mrs. Czernak shrugged in agreement. I put on some gloves and started in on a huge stack of plates next to the sink. Mrs. Czernak went back outside and I was left with Lucy and Sam to make conversation. They told me they liked their teachers at school, that their rooms were clean, they didn't need help with their homework, and their Sunday School homework and memory work was done. I tested them on their memory work after I started the dishwasher. I found that they did know their memory work well, and Lucy offered to wipe the tables as I cleared them and began to do the rest of the dishes by hand.

"Who is that?" I asked Lucy, indicating a picture on the hutch. It was of a gray-haired man in his late thirties or forties, taken probably fifty years ago in black and white.

"That's my grandpa Czernak."

"Your mother's father?"

She nodded, then said, "I don't know where my dad is. He is not home much."

"Where is your grandfather?" Mrs. Czernak had come in by then and was listening to us talking.

Lucy said, "In heaven with the angels. God took him home when I was seven. Now I'm ten. But I remember him. Sam doesn't."

Sam was working intently with crayons and a colorbook in the corner of the kitchen at a little kids' play table.

"Here's his diary." Mrs. Czernak came over and stood by me. She pulled a little book off the top shelf of the hutch. "I want you to have it. We can call it payment for cleaning. My father was a speaker of the Word as you are."

I didn't really want to take a family heirloom but she insisted so I accepted the book and flipped it open. There were no dates or entries about his activities, I saw that right away. There were only notes about Bible passages. One caught my eye: "Genesis 38. The calling of the Gentiles. Tamar became Judah's wife. He had to accept her even if he didn't love her so much (Jacob and Leah) as he ought to have. Joseph on his way to Egypt to preach to the Gentiles. Martin Luther."

"Ma'am," I insisted, shutting the book. "This is a very special book. I can't accept it."

"No, take it," she said almost sharply, then more gently she asked if I wanted more coffee.

I put the diary in my coat pocket, set down my kitchen scrub gloves and went into the living room. Then I got the vacuum out of the closet where Lucy had showed me it was. I was just finishing the vacuuming and was about to wash windows when Sam came in with Mary Ellen.

Mary Ellen watched as I wrapped the cord around the vacuum cleaner and put it away. "You're our babysitter," she said.

"What?" I looked out the window. The minivan was gone. "Your mother left."

"She said you could watch us. She had to go get groceries." By now it was close to the children's bedtime, I thought, it had to be. So I abandoned my window washing idea, read the kids a story, had them get ready for bed and brush their teeth. Then I shepherded them to their rooms and tucked them in. I blessed them and had them repeat prayers with me and we sang the doxology. Then I tiptoed out of their room and went back to my cleaning. I cleaned for another half hour, then laid down on the couch. I'll just shut my eyes for a few minutes, I thought.

Some time later I heard the door click. Mrs. Czernak, loaded with groceries, staggered in. "Thanks for watching the kids," she said. I helped her unload the groceries and put everything away.

"Are you expecting an army?" I had noticed that she bought in bulk and had bought enough food to last a month.

"No. I just forget to grocery shop sometimes. When I knew you were coming over I remembered I needed to go." She smiled at me almost apologetically. "This is what my life is like. If you come visit, you get put to work."

"I don't mind," I said. "But I do need to get home; I have to work tomorrow. Thanks for the diary. And the coffee."

"Come again," she said. "I let you weed if you want. And you can always take home as many tomatoes as you need."

I laughed and thanked her, and then got in my car and drove away through the silent neighborhood. When I got home I read one more page in the diary. It said: "But who may abide the day of his coming? And who shall stand when he appeareth?"

"A good thought," I said out loud, then blew out my candle and went to sleep.

Chapter Four

*I*HAD PROMISED JANET I would be at her assisted living facility
after supper on Tuesday. I bought some goodies from the bakery
at my work and left to go to Janet's straight from work, since I
looked up her address and saw on the internet that the assisted
living place she lived in was only a few blocks from the megastore
I managed at. Janet lived in a hotel-like building, well-kept, with a
big lobby area. Rooms off the lobby held meeting spaces, activity
rooms and music rooms. Some fake plants in pots to the left of
the entryway offered some attempt at natural color and through
a windowed door leading to the back of the building I could see
at least a few flowers surrounding a lawn that was being mowed.

When I got up to the sixth floor where Janet's apartment was,
I noticed wide hallways, more spaces for visiting and group activities, and even a fireplace in a big communal meeting area. Janet
lived towards the end of a hall, and I said hello to three or four
people on my way down the long hall. As I knocked on Janet's door
I thought of my mother.

Janet opened the door, her gray hair in a bun and a pink
apron covering her dress, "Welcome, welcome," she said, greeting me. "What's in the box?" I told her they were goodies and she
pointed to her counter. It was covered with delicious baked goods.
She had probably been baking all day for me.

I stared at the display in dismay but Janet only laughed and
said, "How are we going to eat all this?"

"I don't know," I said. I am not especially short, but I'm not tall either and there was no way I was going to be eating more than a few cookies and a slice of pie. "We could invite more people over. Or," I remembered the communal meeting area, "How about let's bring some of this down to the common room. There are lots of people out there."

As we were making our way down the long hall with the goodies, my phone beeped. With one hand I thumbed through my messages, my other hand carrying my box of goodies. It was a text from someone unfamiliar. It said:

"Are you coming to the deaconate meeting? You're late."

I responded:

"Woops, I forgot. I am doing deaconate work right now, so I won't make the meeting. Who is this?"

The reply came:

"This is Erik, Heidi's husband."

I texted him back:

"I would rather do deaconate work than talk about doing it. Let me know what the meeting minutes are if there are any."

I shut my phone. Janet asked who it was as we set our boxes and plates down in the commons area. I explained.

"I like Erik," she said. "He's very organized."

"Do you think I offended him?" I told her what I had responded and why.

"No. I agree with you. Some people are better at organization and getting things going, others have the gift of just visiting and keeping people company. Both are necessary."

I looked around the room. With my thinning brown hair that was already starting to gray I felt like I fit right in. We found a sofa and chairs and sat down. I asked Janet, "So, do you think I should go to the next deaconate meeting? How do things work around here?"

"No. I don't think it matters if you go. Do you go to any other night meetings?"

I told her about alcoholic family support groups I was trying to help out at, and youth activities that I had heard might benefit from me being there.

Janet thought about that, then said, "Just keep doing what you are doing and keep an open ear if someone comes and talks to you or has questions about what you are up to."

"Yes, Paul says at the beginning of his second letter to the Corinthians that we should comfort people."

I stayed until ten thirty. Janet and I visited with the people in the commons area. I got invitations to craft socials, puzzle evenings and a game evening. I organized one lady's embroidery, did a 500 piece puzzle of a fishing scene with a very silent old black man, watched as one elderly couple showed us how to put a ship together inside a bottle, ate four cookies and a piece of lemon pie, and drank more weak coffee than I had in a long time.

As I drove home I reviewed what Janet had told me. She had talked extensively about many of her neighbors, who they were, who was related to who, what they all did for a living. I wished my mom were healthier; wouldn't it be great if I could have her near me living in a place like that? But she needed round-the-clock care because her mind was going so I knew it would never be possible. Janet had offered to ride with me when I went to visit my mother on Thursday. I didn't think it would work out, but I thought, wow, what a good friend! I was so grateful to her, and to God for preserving her in health so she could be a support to me and others.

I had asked Janet about the Czernaks and shown her the little book Mrs. Czernak had given me. She had smiled knowingly. "Yes, that's just like Grandpa Czernak," she had said. "He had a hard life. All of his children fell away from faith. It must have been difficult but he kept on teaching and studying. He wasn't much for visiting, but his wife was, so she would invite people over and he would just sit in a recliner and watch all the hubbub. I remember more than once his wife would even be loudly debating about religion or politics with someone, and old Mr. Czernak would just listen placidly."

I asked her about the younger Mrs. Czernak, whose house I had just helped clean. Janet explained that Grandpa Czernak's son

Jared had married this woman and they had had three children, then Jared had lost his faith and left her. Grandpa Czernak had lived with the younger Mrs. Czernak and the three children, but then he had passed away a year or two ago. "All his children were there when he died," Janet recalled. "And he pleaded with them to be prepared when God one day rang the bell calling them from this life." Janet said one by one they went out of the room until the only one left was the young Mrs. Czernak and her three children. "He asked them for a blessing, then, his hands still on them blessing them, he died." Janet said young Mrs. Czernak had sang a hymn all alone in the room and then came out where Grandpa Czernak's children were waiting with all the guests who had come with flowers and greetings. Janet had been there.

"You could feel all the guests praying for those children of Grandpa Czernak. We knew what he longed for on their behalf when he died."

"But none of them repented?" I asked.

"No," she said sadly.

"Not yet," I said. "Not then, and not today, but maybe someday."

I thought about that as I looked at my garden in the moonlight when I got home. I got down on my knees and started weeding. I noticed some little animals had come in and eaten some of my fresh vegetables, so I got some wire from the woodshed and put up a fence. Taking a handful of peapods up to the back porch I sat chewing on them a while, watching my few sunflowers wave to the moon in the still air. From a pond nearby I heard frogs croaking. Somewhere down the road a dog barked. The car door of my neighbor slammed as he got home from the early night shift at the factory. My eyes went over my fence again—would it be enough? And it wouldn't keep out bugs. What was I going to do when those got thick?

The covers of the mason jars on the table next to the garden flashed like gold medallions at me. I went inside, read a little, and then looked at my Bible. Just one verse, I thought. I opened to the psalm and began to read, "If God had not been on our side, let Jerusalem now say . . ."

Chapter Five

*T*ODAY WAS WEDNESDAY, THE day I was to go to coffee with Heidi's sister, Amy. I met her at a grocery store down the road from where I lived because there was a coffee bar in the store. Amy had long brown hair pulled back to one side. She was almost scowling as she shook my hand, but she took off her spring coat, ordered a large coffee with an extra shot of espresso, and pulled up a chair across from me next to a group of studying students.

The section of the store we were in played music very softly, and the sound of the shoppers surrounded us so that we were able to talk in private. Amy told me she taught high school art courses. She said she didn't do much art herself—she said she was too critical—but she loved to teach students drawing and sculpture. I told her I would gladly take any clay pots she had as surplus—I was always looking for more creative ways to do my gardening. I asked Amy why Heidi, her sister, hadn't come.

"Oh, I told her she didn't need to."

"Why do you think she wanted you to meet with me?" I asked.

"She wants me to repent, as she says."

"Yes, the Bible says that was the message that the prophets, John the Baptist, Jesus and those who followed him came preaching: 'The kingdom of God is at hand. Repent and believe the gospel.' Do you feel and know your sins—do they trouble you?" I asked her.

"Do you want me to list out my sins?" she responded.

"No. It's just that God creates a stricken conscience; he gives a feeling in a heart of sorrow over one's sins, of knowledge of them. Oftentimes a person can be in this condition of being awakened to the knowledge of their sins—their sins are felt as a burden daily crushing them. This is true godly sorrow that leads to repentance. I ask only if that has been your experience."

"No," she said, glancing over at the shoppers putting their carts away. We sipped our coffees.

I listened to the soft piano music for a while. The students next to us were studying chemistry together, I noticed. Amy fussed with her chipped fingernail and took long gulps of her large coffee. It was almost gone. I said to her, "Are you sure you don't do any art—none at all? I'd like to see any paintings or sculptures you have done."

She thought a moment, twirling some strands of long hair on her fingers. "Well, I do have some paintings. Three, in fact. I had dreams of myself out on an island alone, where the rocks were all fiery red or dark as cooled lava. So I got up in the middle of the night and painted my dreams. Here, let me show you." She got out her phone and I looked at pictures of her paintings. I couldn't see much detail, the screen was too small for that, but I saw all kinds of red and red-brown colors, and then one small figure, on the edge by a shore of vast blue.

"I don't put much stock in dreams," I said, "Unless I have a very compelling reason to do so, but I think that I see that these paintings show a lonely person. Are you lonely?"

There was a silence, such a one as if someone was straining to hear what was being said. But besides the silently reading students, the tables around us were empty. Finally Amy answered me: "Somewhat. Who isn't at times? But I go to Heidi's quite often and visit her and her husband and children. Well, her husband is seldom there—actually Heidi seems lonelier than me. I have my work, which is taxing, but it keeps me very busy so I don't have time to be lonely. Heidi's husband is always gone—she needs him and he is never there. I try to visit her and help but she misses him a great deal. I know."

"Where is he?"

"He travels for his work; he's a business trainer, and a very successful one. And when he gets home he's at workshops, camps, meetings, political group discussions, and he also does community service." She stirred her coffee, though it was getting cold now. "Quite a bit of community service, actually."

"Thanks for telling me that; I've never met him, exactly, but he sounds like a busy guy."

"Well, he does have a family, too; he might want to remember that."

"Do you have family besides Heidi?"

"Yes, many other siblings, but most of them don't live around here. What about you?"

I told her about my mother whose mind was going, who lived in a nursing home two hours away. Then Amy asked me what books I liked to read. I told her I was a little like Erik, Heidi's husband, a goer and not much of a reader. She laughed. "You'll get along good with him then."

I nodded. "Why don't I text you next time I go to Heidi's, or to Heidi and Erik's, and we can all visit together."

She agreed and we parted, her to home and met to pick up a few things from the store before Bible Class. As I went through the toothpaste aisle I thought about her paintings. I should have had her forward a copy to me, I thought. But dreams, even though they appear many times in the Bible, are not something I put much weight to. I guess I've read Luther enough to know that it's better and safer to stick to the spoken and written Word of God and the sure voice of the Spirit in the congregation than to give too much credence to doubtful dreams. Sometimes they support and uplift, or reveal something to us, just as nature reveals the majesty of God to us, but it is through the revealed Word that we come to God and know his will perfectly by the Spirit. I wished I had had the courage to talk more with Amy about serious matters, but I encouraged myself in this that she was willing to talk again and that she and Heidi were close and had good communication between them. Something we all need. The words of 1 Corinthians 1 came to mind: "I have planted, Apollos has watered, but it is God who has given the increase."

Chapter Six

---

*O*N THE WAY TO Bible Class that night I admired the tall trees in the suburbs through which I drove. It was a wealthy area for the most part but at times I drove past areas that looked as if a storm had gone through the neighborhood and beaten it up. But the blighted areas soon gave way to expensively built modern homes and then I was at the church.

I was a little late, but I sneaked into one of the back rows just as the Bible Class leader began. He drew pictures as he told this story. "Imagine," he said, "a courtroom. In this courtroom God is judge. Jesus is the lawyer and you are the one on trial. The judge has read all your crimes and faults. Jesus has pleaded with the judge that nevertheless you ought to be let free because of his own suffering and death and resurrection victory. The judge has just declared you innocent, having been pleased with the pleading voice of Jesus—his wounds have convinced the judge to let you go free. Suddenly the door of the courtroom opens. In walks one of the henchmen of the enemy of souls. He begins to argue and accuse: 'This person is proud. This person has many faults. This person has done many sins, sins that many other people remember. This person causes offence.'"

I looked around the congregation. All were listening. Over to my left a few rows up, Heidi sat watching the presenter, this time with her husband Erik. Only a few of her youngest children were with her. The older ones had gone into the basement for the children's Bible Class.

The Bible Class leader began to talk about the forgiveness of sins, about carrying one another with forgiveness and patience. He quoted from Ephesians 4 and 5: "Let all bitterness, and wrath, and anger, and clamor, and evil speaking, be put away from you, with all malice. And be ye kind one to another, tenderhearted, forgiving one another, even as God for Christ's sake hath forgiven you. Be ye therefore followers of God, as dear children; and walk in love, as Christ also hath loved us, and hath given himself for us an offering and a sacrifice to God for a sweet-smelling savor. But fornication, and all uncleanness, or covetousness, let it not be once named among you, as becometh saints; neither filthiness, nor foolish talking, nor jesting, which are not convenient: but rather giving of thanks. For this ye know, that no whoremonger, nor unclean person, nor covetous man, who is an idolater, hath any inheritance in the kingdom of Christ and of God." After a bit he asked if there were any questions or comments. There were. As people spoke I learned a good deal and reflected that this was a wonderful way to do Bible Class. I thought about what I might say if I took the microphone for a speaking turn but nothing came to mind so I just listened.

We sang a hymn about Christ's love and patience, then the leader closed the Bible Class with a prayer. After the closing hymns and announcements everybody went for coffee and rolls. I got in line next to Heidi and told her about my conversation with her sister Amy. She was pleased that Amy had showed up and we decided that in two weeks we would try to meet at Heidi's for lunch and visiting.

I had gotten my coffee and roll and had spotted Shelly and Freddie sitting at a table on the far side of the room. I was about to go sit with them when Erik turned to me and greeted me.

"So," he said, "You didn't come to the deaconate committee meeting. Do you plan to go to board meetings or any other kinds of meetings?" His tone was rather cold and I took a step back from him, almost bumping into a stroller.

"I'll take them all into consideration as each one comes up on my schedule," I said, taking a measured sip of my coffee. "James says that he who sees to do good and does not do it, to him it is sin."

Erik looked at me for a minute as we stood there. Then he looked down and contemplated his roll. His tone a little thawed, he said, "But don't you think these meetings should take precedence over other things? It is the work of the kingdom we are doing and planning for."

I took a bite of my roll, scanning the room for a minute. Then I said, "Jesus said: This is the work that you do: Believe on me. My place, I feel now as I always have, is among the people." I didn't tell him that I had been on committees before and sometimes they had gone well, but sometimes also contentiously. "I prefer one-on-one visiting. I like to help people that way, and I keep out of trouble easier," I confessed.

"Well there is a big meeting coming up on Saturday where we are going to discuss youth problems; will you be there?" he asked.

"Sure. As long as some youth or youths or someone else doesn't call in the meantime and ask for me to come help them. Or, if I feel I am needed more elsewhere. Jesus says to visit those in prison." Erik seemed uninterested in what I was saying but I pressed on. "Sometimes people are in the prison of their own mind, or they are a shut-in. I can't ignore them. I have to visit them, and yes, I'll neglect meetings to do that work. Others can attend meetings."

Erik shrugged. "It starts at 8am and will probably last until about four." He told me it would be held at the church and that there would be a pizza meal served at noon. Then Heidi, who had been listening, said that if I decided to go, I ought to come over to her house for supper afterwards. I thanked them both and then looked back at the table where Shelly and Freddie were sitting. It was full. I studied the room. One of the elders' tables had an open spot right near Janet. I went and sat in it, greeting everyone.

Janet introduced me to everyone. They were talking about various people who needed visitors. I took out my notebook and began writing them down. I had tentatively booked my Friday evening to visit a sick person and was just writing in my calendar to book myself for visiting an elderly shut-in some other day when the man next to me took note of me. "You're rather young to be at the elders' table," he remarked.

"Yes," I said, "But look here, now I might have something to do Friday night and it looks like I'm not going to be going to part of a Saturday meeting in order to go visit this Auntie Ella. Do you know her?"

"Yes, she's ninety-three. Her mind is sharp but her body is sickly and has been for years." He put another roll on my plate. "She likes singing, and visiting, and she likes to talk about faith. She's been through a good deal. Of her family she is the only one who survived in faith after the last heresy."

"Really? She probably knows a lot about those days—but I bet you do too, Max."

"Yes. The lesson tonight touched me deeply, because that was how it was—that is how the enemy works to destroy souls. He causes accusations, lies, envying, and bitterness to spring up as an evil root. It consumes faith away. And it is all done under pretenses of love." He indicated my notebook and the names I had taken down. "Be careful with that. Don't ever start categorizing Christians as those who are truly believing and those who are not really believing as well as the others—it's dangerous. King David got into this 'counting spirit' at the end of his life and many fell away in that spiritual battle."

I thanked Max. I agreed with him because I myself struggled with categorizing people into good and better Christians. For example if I went to visit a large family where it looked like they gladly accepted children, were calm and hospitable, and had many visitors, I often compared these kinds of families to other families. Some families I visited had a morose atmosphere, others were very negative and critical, others seemed lenient or too severe. I judged them all harshly in my mind, I felt. "It's a struggle," I told Max.

"It helps to read the Bible," he encouraged me. "For example, look at the life of David. His own family had so many problems, even murder and rape happened among his own children Amnon, Tamar, and Absalom. There's nothing new under the sun."

"True," I said, glancing over to where Shelly had been sitting. She was gone. Freddie was gone, too. I wondered where the younger people or older singles were going. I texted Freddie to ask him. He didn't respond immediately so I visited more with the elders. Janet was talking about some upcoming music festivals she and some others were trying to organize. Then a woman, Carole, came by and told me I needed to prepare lessons to teach eighth grade Sunday School every Sunday. I thanked her and chatted with her a while to learn how Sunday School was done in this area.

I was curious to ask Shelly her opinion of my conversation with Erik, so I texted Freddie again:

"Where is everyone going?"

He responded:

"To my house. Welcome. We're having another bonfire."

Just then a pastor brother, Donald, pulled up a chair next to me. "Edmund," he said, "There have been many people lately with many questions about the accepting of children. A few of us are going to meet in the sacristy now to discuss this and we'd like for you to come."

Puzzled and interested I followed him to the sacristy. There were five other men in the room and Donald introduced me to them all. Two wore suits, the others were dressed in business casual, as I was. I recognized one of the men as the one who had led the Bible Class that evening. He was sitting with his head down, looking at an open Bible. It didn't seem like a formal meeting. I asked about that.

"No. I just looked around and saw who was here tonight," a middle-aged man named Mortin said. "I figured we might as well discuss the matter of accepting children and how we might address questions and concerns in this area." He stood up. The rest of the men were seated. I stayed standing, leaning against the wall.

The man who had led the Bible Class said, "All right. But I have to go soon to help my wife with the kids."

"Fair enough," Mortin said.

"Wait," I said. "Why is this issue discussed and others are not? Am I free to bring up other issues?"

"Sure." Mortin sat down. "Go ahead."

I turned towards him. "I've noticed and heard that some of the young men have a sensual way of treating the young women. It shows up in their way of talking especially, but also in the general way the girls get treated, both before courtship, in courtship, and in marriage." I felt silly talking but the matter was truly on my mind and I couldn't stop my mouth from going on talking. "Boaz warned the young men in his day not to hurt Ruth or treat her poorly. Also we know that one of David's sons, Amnon, became so involved in sensuousness that he lost his faith and even raped his own sister. Balaam also fell and many with him, because of fornication, as it says in Numbers 31 and 1 Corinthians 10 and other places. And actually, the matter of viewing women in an exclusively sensual way relates to the matter of accepting children."

"Maybe you could explain that," said Mortin hesitantly.

"How?" asked the man who had led the Bible class lesson, who I later learned was a cousin of Shelly's; his name was Lev.

"It is about the marriage relationship. My point is, just as we in faith are willing-hearted and do all things out of love, and not because of desire for reward or fear of punishment, so also ought the marriage relationship be." I paused, feeling my single state very keenly. "That is what Scripture teaches."

"So these are problems that you see happening?" Mortin sounded even more upset. Lev motioned Mortin to be quiet and urged me to elaborate.

"Girls and married women don't report abuse. It's so shameful to them. Neither do our young men. And even in very candid and free sessions of marriage counseling these matters often remain unspoken of—but they cause a great deal of harm. I am just thinking of the dangerous places on the internet and how quickly a man's view of woman changes when he gets caught up in sensuousness."

Morton stood up, setting his Bible down in front of him and going over to where the communion dishes were stacked. He scrutinized them for a moment and then turned back around.

Since he still didn't say anything, I said, "I heard a presentation in my local area recently about accepting children. In it the presenter said that the matter must be considered in the context of what God's Word says about marriage in its entirety. My heart said amen to that presentation."

"I have to leave," Lev said, shutting his cell phone off. "My wife just texted me. She needs help with finding our toddler."

Some of the other men stood up, too. One of them, who was very young and had fair hair and a dark purple suit said, "We just started."

"What should we do now, Mortin?" Donald asked.

"Why don't we talk next week after Bible Class."

I nodded, and the others agreed this might be a good idea. As I went out of the room Lev put his hand on my shoulder and squeezed. The pastor brother in the dark purple suit asked me to come over and visit sometime. Mortin watched us pensively across the room. Donald looked confused. I sighed to myself and wondered what Shelly would say about the meeting.

The church was almost empty, coffee lunch had winded down, and the ushers were shutting off lights. There was no sign of Freddie or Shelly.

I checked my texts. There was one from Freddie:

"Where ARE you?"

I texted back:

"At church still. I'll have to come by another time."

I chatted with Donald a while outside in the parking lot about the building project he was working on. It was getting close to midnight when I got in my car and drove home. When I got home I watered plants and went straight to bed. As I drifted off to sleep Paul's words were the last words on my mind: "Put ye on the Lord Jesus Christ, and make no provisions for the flesh, to fulfill the lusts thereof."

Chapter Seven

────────◆────────

EVEN THOUGH I GOT home so late I couldn't sleep. After turning
restlessly a half hour I got up. I sat at a little wooden table next
to my bed and opened my Bible. The way Donald had acted in the
meeting remained in my mind. He seemed confused. Mortin had
seemed disturbed and upset but Donald seemed confused. Why? I
wasn't confused, myself, on the issue—or was I? I had always seen
from the Scriptures that it is the man's responsibility to treat the
woman right. In Timothy it says to young men that they are to
treat all women as their sisters. I paged through to the life of David
and read about Amnon and Tamar. Just as with Bathsheba, the text
put no blame or responsibility on the woman. It was all put on the
man. I flipped over to Thessalonians. There again Paul warns about
keeping one's "vessel" in honor. Again the responsibility for correct
behavior and attitude is left especially with the man. The same idea
is in the incident about Reuben in Genesis as well as in chapters
5 to 7 of Paul's first letter to the Corinthians. I turned the pages of
the Bible randomly for a while, skimming, but I simply couldn't
see anything that showed the primary responsibility for the right
relationship between men and women in sensual matters to rest
with the woman.

Was I missing something? About four years back I had been
courting a girl and this was one of the reasons we had ended the
courtship. She and I had disagreed vehemently about her brother.
I got to know her brother pretty well and I saw how he was with

women. He was married, and he made comments about how different women looked, he said things about their pasts, and yet he was very conservative about his own daughters. He even would call them bad names if they dressed even a little too loosely. I didn't know all that happened in their home but I tried to talk many times to his wife. She remained subdued and seemed so trodden down in spirit. I remember feeling so helpless and not knowing how to help the situation. The girl I had courted defended her brother. She said that his wife was not troubled and was not hiding anything. I remember her making disdainful comments about some girls we both knew. I myself thought of them as troubled and sometimes abused when I saw how they dressed to objectify themselves. But the woman I was courting didn't see them as young and taken advantage of. She didn't agree with me that they did not understand what they were doing when they put all their worth in their sensual appeal. It was an odd situation, too, because the woman I was courting was herself so beautiful. She seemed to have sailed through her teen years and young adult years without one problem. I remember trying to bring her down to a women's shelter once so she could hear how some of the lives of the women there had been—from childhood their surroundings had all been drugs and sex and rock and roll. They had seen very little that was wholesome. Pain had come to them at an early age. The men in their lives had not been taught not to look at a woman sensuously unless it was their wife and it was after marriage. The girl I courted listened to the women's stories but as we drove home I asked her if she wanted to go back again and she said, "No, I prefer not to be around those kinds of people; they bring me down."

I shut my Bible and laid back down. An hour had gone by. My swirling thoughts slowly calmed as I prayed and then thought about gardening. I enviously remembered Mrs. Czernak's garden. I should find some time to weed my garden tomorrow morning before work, I thought. How were my tomato plants? Should I stop by the nursery next week? Because I've got to drive out to my mom's nursing home right after work.

What would other people have said about the meeting we had had tonight? The Scripture came to mind, "Do all things without quarrelling . . ."

Chapter Eight

*T*HE NEXT AFTERNOON, THURSDAY, I left work and drove directly out of the city towards a small town about two hours east. My mom was in a nursing home there and I asked the nurses at the front desk how she was before I went to find her. They said she had been well since I had been there a little over a week ago. They said she didn't wander around, she generally stayed in her room or went into the activity room to watch people do puzzles or visit. I asked if she got many visitors and the nurse said, "She's got a couple right now. Her visitors do a good job with her. Since she doesn't communicate much, because the disease she has is getting so bad, they sing with her. This is good for her. It's something she can join in with."

I left the nurse's desk and went to my mom's room. Pictures of me were tacked onto a bulletin board. Embroidered verses and country scenes cluttered the walls. Mom was propped up in bed with a yellow patterned dress on. I went to greet her and she seemed to recognize me a little, but I wasn't sure. I held her hand and turned to her visitors. It was Harold and Monica, an elderly couple from my home congregation, the one I had grown up in. I greeted them and embraced them. They held songbooks so I suggested we continue singing if that is what they had been doing.

We sang for a half hour and mom and I shared a songbook. She seemed glad but tired. She drifted in and out of slumber as we sang, and finally nodded off completely. I turned to Harold and Monica.

"Greetings from Janet," I said.

Harold thanked me, then said, "I notice you are clutching your Bible there—open it and say a few words if you are of a mind to."

"No." I set my Bible down on top of the songbook and ran my hands through my hair. "Is my consternation so obvious?" We were speaking softly because Mom was sleeping right next to me, but I knew she would sleep through anything. I went over to the CD player in the corner and put on some organ music on low volume.

"Sit down," Harold said. "What's on your mind?"

"I don't know. Faith and reason, I guess. I want more understanding." I suddenly realized this was one of the matters bothering my heart most. "Is that wrong? It says in James in the first chapter to ask God for wisdom."

"Yes." Harold opened my Bible. He turned to first Corinthians the first chapter and read, "That in everything ye are enriched by him, in all utterance, and in all knowledge." Then he turned to Ephesians the first chapter and read, "Wherein he hath abounded toward us in all wisdom and understanding." And then he turned to Philippians, the first chapter and read, "And this I pray, that your love may abound yet more and more in knowledge and in all judgment." Then Harold said, "Do you want me to continue?"

I smiled at him and Monica. "I get the point. Yes, then, the answer is yes, I should want more understanding."

"The Bible talks about asking for understanding or knowledge and it also uses the word which is translated 'discernment.' It's a good thing to ask for understanding so that you can discern what things are to be approved of and what things are to be discarded. Is there a specific matter you're struggling with?"

I laughed. "Marriage, in fact."

"You're courting? Congratulations and God's blessings."

I held up my hand. "No, not now, no." I told them about the meeting the previous night.

Harold listened carefully and then slowly flipped through the pages of the Bible and read from the first chapter of Colossians. "For this cause we also, since the day we heard it, do not cease to pray for you, and to desire that ye might be filled with the knowledge of his will in all wisdom and spiritual understanding." He shut the book. "This is what my hope is for you, Edmund. I can't say that I have anything else to offer other than to give attendance to reading and prayer. Maybe soon there will be a congregational discussion on some of these topics and we can hear what the Spirit says to the churches even in these difficult matters."

"Yes." I straightened Mom's bedspread and fluffed her pillow. "You should tell me some time about how you two fell in love and began to court."

Monica laughed, her faded blue eyes sparkling. "We began to court, then I fell in love," she said.

Harold gave her a surprised look and then realized she was teasing. "Really," he asked her. "I am sure I fell in love with you first and then had to convince you over the course of a year to fall in love with me."

"Maybe that's the way it went," she said solemnly. "I just remember a rather long courtship. It was three years because you were in the service."

"True. Things were much different back then." And he began to tell me about how there had been chaperones, how most of their being together as a couple had been in homes and at church. Monica told me about the first time they had sat together in services and how important it was.

She exhorted me: "Stay among people, keep close to the voice of the congregation. Be in the home of her parents and hear their advice. Take Moses in chapter two of Exodus as a good example. Gather at the well of grace. Forgive one another."

I tried to backtrack, insisting I wasn't courting anyone, but Harold only winked and said, "Well, who said you were courting? You're the one who keeps bringing it up. We're just giving you advice in case you have interest in someone and are considering courtship."

I rolled my eyes in good humor and picked up a songbook. Monica picked one up too. "Let's sing a wedding song," she said. "Just in case we need to practice." I smiled at her and picked a song. As we sang it, Mom woke up. But we just kept singing and I moved the songbook over to where mom could see it. Her frail voice joined in, "Blest be the tie that binds our hearts in Christian love."

Chapter Nine

MY DRIVE HOME WAS on a route I had never taken. It was ten o'clock and I was passing through gray and somewhat ramshackle suburbs when I realized I had been around these parts before. Up ahead of me would be the women's shelter I had visited with that girl those many years ago—if it was still here. The streets and buildings were old and I felt the creeps crawl up my neck for a minute but then I saw the soft lights of the upstairs rooms of the old Victorian house that served as a women's shelter. I noticed the entryway light on, too, and as I pulled up and parked, through the cut-glass decorated windows I saw a woman seated at the front desk. Was it anyone I knew? I got out of my car and went in. The woman looked up. I didn't recognize her. She wore lots of strongly colored make-up. She motioned me towards a chair with a hand covered with bangles half-way to her elbow. Her smile was big behind the deep red lipstick she wore.

"I am Edmund," I said.

"Betty," she replied. "How can I help you?"

"I'd like to volunteer, if you need any volunteers. Either here or at another facility."

Betty nodded and handed me an application, some empty folders to write on, and a pen. As I sat in the waiting room I could hear voices coming down the hall towards me.

"Let go of my arm." The woman's voice was distinct and so loud I could make out what she was saying, even though she seemed a long ways away.

The other voice answered the shrill woman calmly in words I couldn't understand.

"Where's Shelly?" the shrill-voiced woman demanded.

The other voice murmured a reply.

Then the loud woman spoke again, on a sob, "Yes, Shelly Bonn. Where is she?"

I couldn't hear the reply again and I realized I was clutching my pen and staring down towards the hallway. Betty had stepped out of the room. Footsteps came closer to the reception room, empty except for me. I bent down to finish my application. After a minute, feeling eyes on me, I looked up. There was a forty-ish woman with short tangled brown hair, a darker complexion and dull blue eyes. Her hands were ringless except for one big turquoise mood ring on the pinky of her left hand. She wore three necklaces that were not bulky but made her look a little more dressed up even though she just had on a cotton tank top and jeans. Her cowboy boots had run down under the scuffed hem of her jeans.

I smiled at her. "Shelly Bonn?" I asked.

"You know her?" Her voice was raspy.

"Yes. She's a good friend."

"She volunteers here. But I guess I thought she would be here tonight and she's not."

"I can give her a message."

"No, that's okay. She'll be back."

The woman remained standing and as I studied her, I wondered how old she really was. Probably thirty, not forty. "Do you live around here?" I asked.

"No. I live wherever I can find a place."

"Any kids?"

The woman's voice sharpened. "No." Then she crossed her arms across the front of her teal tank top. "Actually, it's none of your business. What are you doing here anyway?"

"I'm going to try to volunteer."

"But you're a man."

"So. I can do yard work. Or errands, or even fundraising."

"If you're friends with Shelly, maybe you'd be a good counselor."

"I'm licensed to counsel, actually, but it has been a few years since I've counseled in a place like this."

"So counsel now. Tell me what to do."

I put my application into one of the folders and wrote my name on the label of the folder. I got up and walked towards the woman, went around her, and set the folder on Betty's desk.

"What's your name?" I asked, as gently as I could.

"Rachel."

"Hello, Rachel, what do you want to talk about?"

"You tell me."

"What does Shelly do? How does she help you?"

Rachel was silent a long while. I listened to the old clock ticking in the room and noticed how strange the seventies style rag rug and the institutional orange plastic chairs looked in a room trimmed with beautiful old Victorian-era wood work.

Finally the woman said, "She doesn't say anything. She just takes walks with me and listens."

"So I will listen to you. Go ahead."

"Maybe some other time."

Then she said, "In your Bible, it says it's Dinah's fault that Shechem did what he did to her."

"No, it doesn't," I said. "Genesis 34."

"Right." She smirked.

"Look at the text. Dinah is not the actor, the aggressor. Shechem is."

She raised her eyebrows. "Right."

"We can't even tell what her reaction was."

"Really?" She looked interestedly at me. The moon shined in the small yard outside. Owls hooted.

"Just as with Bathsheba," I said.

"Really?" She looked confused.

"Because it doesn't matter. The man is at fault. The woman had no choice."

"They rarely do," she said. Then she turned to go.

"No, stay, talk to me."

She turned back, and sat down. We began to discuss the programs that the shelter ran, when some of the sessions were held, and how beneficial they were or how they might be improved. When Betty came back in the room she picked up my folder and flipped through it, glancing back and forth at times between me and Rachel. When Rachel and I yawned at the same time, we both laughed and I told them I had to work in the morning so I had better go.

"I'll be in touch," Betty said.

"I doubt he would work out," Rachel told her, motioning towards me.

"Give me a chance," I said. "That's all I ask for." Then I opened the brass-latched heavy old door and went out into the night. I sang all the way home.

When I got home, I thought about my garden. But, too tired to even go out back and quickly check the fences, I read one verse from the Song of Solomon before I nodded off to sleep, "Let him kiss me with the kisses of his mouth: for thy love is better than wine."

Chapter Ten

———◁◦▷———

*T*HE NEXT DAY WAS Friday. Work was hectic and the whole day I kept worrying about how the evening would go. As soon as my shift was over I got in my car and sat there, texting Freddie.

"Where is everyone going tonight?"

He texted me back:

"Janet is having some of us older single people over later tonight, at 9 or later. You're welcome to come."

I stopped at the VA hospital on the way home to try to visit one of my uncles. He wasn't available for visiting but they said to come back; he needed visitors. I left him a card and drove home, planning my next gardening moves. When I pulled in the driveway I noticed a small car parked on the street in front of my house. On the steps stood the pastor brother from the Wednesday night meeting—the one who had worn the dark purple suit. He was reading the newspaper that lay there. I hollered greetings to him to get his attention. He put the paper down.

"How long have you been waiting?" I asked.

"Not long. And I am Micah. I don't think we were ever formally introduced. I hope you don't mind me dropping in."

"Not at all. What seems to be the problem?" I asked as I unlocked the door and let us in. No garden fence-checking yet, I thought.

He sat on the rocking chair in the kitchen and I made coffee and poured juice for us. "No specific problem," he said. "I've just been thinking a lot about the meeting Wednesday night."

Honesty is the best policy, my father had always liked to tell me. I said, "Let me be frank, I have learned to be leery of meetings. Some kinds of meetings at least. These days I try to ask what the purpose and meaning of a meeting is before I go into one. Paul says in Acts 20 that he preached openly and publicly from house to house. Nothing invite-only. It also says in the Bible to rebuke things publicly, so all may learn, and fear."

"And you forgot to do that on Wednesday night," Micah said.

"Yes. I try to be careful that I am not lending my presence to a meeting that is about listing the sins of other people. I found that this got to be a problem a few years back when I did youthwork all summer. Older people would call a meeting and talk about the faults and reputations of younger people. Sometimes this has happened in other settings, too. Sometimes meetings have been called in which one person's faults and sins are the main agenda item, and that person may or may not even be present at the meeting. I do not want to be a part of such goings on, not even by just physically being present even if I don't join in speaking at the meeting."

"So that is why you were wary at first in the meeting on Wednesday night."

"Yes. But I realized quickly that it was about some questions people have been having concerning matters of conscience and the intent was to discuss the matters and give instruction and encouragement to each other." I gave him a cup of juice and a mug of coffee. "Something the entire congregation could benefit from."

"It was a nice meeting, but too short." He got out his Bible. "I was reading more in the Scripture and thought I could speak with you one-on-one and face-to-face."

"That's good. What exactly about?"

He shook his head, then marked his page with his finger and motioned with his Bible as he talked. "I'm 42 and I've been married only three years. I have two kids. My wife and I have had many conversations about women and men, how the young girls dress, how the young boys are, and other similar issues. Now you seem to be saying that, well—I can't describe it. But you sound like my wife."

"It's not me saying anything," I said. "I don't see how one can get around Scripture in this matter. In the Bible, whenever there is an actual woman, and not a metaphor, this is where the primary responsibility for right relationships between men and women lies—on the man."

"Okay, but look at our world today. Think how difficult it is for men."

"True. Remember Potiphar's wife and Joseph. And also I can't help but feel there is a great warning in the examples of Esau and Solomon, who fell away from faith by being overwhelmed with sensuousness, taking many wives and concubines. In Noah's time it says that they took wives as many as they chose—that is, they saw a woman and took her. They disregarded marriage, chastity, decency. In the Bible, to take a woman means to take her as a wife. The Bible shows how closely linked official marriage is to physical marriage—they are essentially the same thing. Thus, taking many wives means knowing many women as you only ought to know a wife. This is why Jesus allows divorce in case of adultery. It is because in adultery, because of the act that has taken place, you now are considering not one marriage, but two marriages, one that is both official and physical, and one that is just a physical marriage."

"What do you mean?"

"I mean this is why Jesus says that divorce is allowed when adultery is involved. Once adultery has taken place, the man has two wives. Not one. One he is officially and physically married to, and the other he is only physically married to."

"Oh."

"Look in the gospels. You will see how Jesus treated women, all women. He was very kind to them. He did as it says in Timothy to do, he treated the older women as mothers and the younger women as sisters, and I don't think it mattered to him what they were wearing—they all got treated respectfully."

"That's what my wife says. She says the line, 'Some women are just asking for it,' is totally wrong."

"She's right." I set down my coffee cup. "But I am hoping I have a correct understanding of the matter myself, so if you read that through," I indicated the Bible in his hand, "And find that I err, you have to tell me."

He promised to do so and we talked for a while more about women and men, and his wife, and about marriage and what Luther said about marriage, how he so highly praised it. I told Micah about my disastrous attempt at courtship and asked him to pray for me. We blessed one another and I brought him out back and said, "Do you mind if I check my fences while we talk?"

"No, I have to go soon anyway, Edmund," He said. So I promised him tomatoes when they came in, and then he walked back into my house. I heard the front door open and close. A minute later, the doorbell rang. I set down my trowel and went in.

My front steps when I opened the door were empty. I turned to my left and saw a beautiful young woman admiring my flowers. She turned as she heard me, "Oh, good evening, Mr.—What's your last name?"

"Call me Edmund," I said, shaking her hand and inviting her in. She had on a brief skirt with a halter top and no spring jacket. She had small sparkling emeralds in her ears, light make-up and her long black hair was loose around her bare shoulders.

"I'm Rachelle," she said. "Amy and Heidi's sister. I should have warned you I was coming, but I came into town today and Amy told me that I might enjoy visiting you. She had to work late, and Heidi is at a baby shower."

Micah and I had not drunk the entire pot of coffee. I offered her a cup, which she declined. I gave her water and poured myself another cup. It was strong but lukewarm.

I stood behind the counter and invited her to sit in the rocking chair in the kitchen. She declined and told me she had a business office job at which she sat all day, so she liked to stand. "Do you mind if I pace?" she joked, "When I'm as restless as this I tend to pace."

She skimmed the headlines of the newspaper that was sitting on my counter and I noticed she had finely done nails. I wondered what kind of work she did, but instead I asked, "What are you restless about?"

She turned lovely brown eyes towards me and then looked away quickly. I waited. One of my best friends, a middle-aged ordained pastor, had told me that few things in counseling were as effective as patient waiting. I had learned over the years to fight my natural inclination to want to talk. Now I leaned on the counter and sipped my tepid coffee and hoped my silence was taken as it was meant to be: warm and inviting.

Rachelle set down the newspaper and began to pace up and down my little kitchen. She had taken off her high heels and they were lined up next to my slippers in the doorway.

"Rachelle," I said tentatively after quite a few minutes had gone by. "I want you to know I'm glad you came. I want you to visit me any time—we should become friends—I hope we do. Just so you know though, I don't counsel women alone. So next time let's go to your sister's or to a public place."

Rachelle froze in her pacing and locked her gaze on my face. I looked down into my coffee but I could feel her staring at me. "Are you afraid of me?" she asked.

"No. I just have been told that it's better to counsel women with another woman, or at least another person present."

"Now that's what I call old-fashioned."

I waited again for almost three minutes. Finally, since she had begun pacing again, I asked her, "You haven't told me why you came. I am assuming you've discussed whatever is bothering you with Heidi. Am I right?"

"Yes."

"Should I call her and talk to her?"

"No. Maybe this wasn't such a good idea to come over to your house like this."

"No, it's fine. I also have a friend, Shelly. I could call her and you might find it easier to talk to her. She's a young single woman like you."

"Actually, I'm married." She saw me looking at her empty ring finger and said, "We're separated. He's actually part of the reason I came." She came and stood directly across from me, putting her perfectly manicured hands on the counter.

I waited, smoothing the countertop with my hands. I sneaked a glance at the clock. It was almost 9:30. Finally I said, "Rachelle, let's go in the living room and listen to music. You can tell me about your job. I'm quite interested in what you do for a living, actually."

She assented and I put some soft piano music on. It was almost completely dark outside so I lit a dim lamp by the sofa and invited her to sit. She sat with her legs curled up under her, drinking lemon water. I sat down in a chair next to her and listened as she told me about her career in the corporate world. She had no children, and now she had no husband to come home to either, so she immersed herself in high finance. We talked about the stock market, retirement planning, and the direction her company was going. An hour went by quickly and I realized I wasn't going to be seeing Janet or Shelly or Freddie or any of the others tonight.

Rachelle was a vivid talker. And she knew her stuff. I got out my portfolio and had her go through my finances and give me advice. "Free advice is always welcome," she teased me. But what she said to me made a lot of sense.

Seeing her yawn I asked her if I should make another pot of coffee. She declined again, drank more water, and asked about my garden. Noticing the time again, I tried a direct question, "Rachelle, I'll tell you about my garden if you tell me why you came to visit me."

"Oh, it was nothing," she said flippantly. "But I gave you advice on your home, your finances, and your taxes. You owe it to me to teach me now about gardening."

"I'm an amateur," I insisted, but obliged her. I wasn't going to get anything out of her tonight at least.

After another half hour of talking, I heard my phone beep. It was a text from Heidi:

"Rachelle is over at your place?"

I responded:

"Yes."

She wrote back:

"Oh, did she say why she came?"

I responded:

"No, but next time she wants to visit me why don't you come with? I don't counsel women alone without another person present. She took me by surprise."

Heidi texted:

"That's Rachelle. Beautiful and impetuous."

Rachelle watched me as I texted good night to Heidi and shut off my phone. "Was that Heidi or Amy?" she asked.

"Heidi," I smiled.

"It figures. I better go now. But thanks so much. I don't know when I last had such an enjoyable evening."

"The pleasure was all mine," I said, and followed her out the door to her car. As we went down the sidewalk, a sleek gray sports car pulled up behind her Toyota. Rachelle got into her car and pulled away from the curb. I turned to the sports car. It was Mortin.

He watched Rachelle's car retreat down the street and then came and greeted me and said, "You live right by everyone and everything. Visitors come often?"

"So far, yes," I said. "I hope it continues."

He noted my dirty hands. "Am I keeping you from something?"

"No."

"I just have a minute and wanted to ask you in person to come to the meeting next Wednesday. I'm bringing some friends in from another area. It should be a good discussion."

I motioned towards the house. "Come in and talk."

"No," he said. "That was Rachelle, wasn't it?"

"Yes," I said.

He kicked at the grass by the curb for a minute with his expensive business shoes.

"I have served at weddings before," he said. "And there's something so beautiful about a couple coming down the aisle towards you about to be joined in holy matrimony and they're both in-nocent. It's a precious matter."

"I've never served at a wedding," I said. "But there's something so beautiful about watching a couple go down the aisle together whose sins are forgiven. And you know they're both innocent of all sin. Sin that nobody can even remember anymore."

"Really," Mortin said. He made as if to go up the path towards my house. Then his hands fell to his side and he said, "It's going to be an important discussion. I hope you come."

"Thanks," I said, and greeted him good night.

After he left I went upstairs to my attic telescope and con-sidered the stars for half an hour. Then I read the Bible for a few minutes. I was not scheduled for sermon for two weeks but I read the different texts for the Easter season anyway. Then I turned to the Psalms and read this last psalm before I turned in for the night: "When I consider the heavens, the work of thy hands, what is man that thou art mindful of him . . ."

Chapter Eleven

———◄○►———

I T WAS EIGHT IN the morning and most of the front benches in the sanctuary were full when I arrived at the Saturday youth meeting. I slid into one of the middle benches next to Donald. I saw Erik and Mortin and Lev and Micah all near the front row.

My phone beeped just as the powerpoint presentation was beginning. The text was from Freddie:

"Where are you?"

I answered him:

"I'm in a meeting at church."

Freddie:

"I thought we were going to visit Aunt Ella."

Me:

"When, though? Right now?"

Freddie:

"Yes, it's a two and a half hour drive."

Me:

"Oh, wow."

Freddie:

"So we leave now, get there before noon and stay for a few hours, then drive home after supper."

Me:

"OK. Let's go. I'm on my way over to your house right now."

I left the church, glad that I was towards the back. When I got to the Bonn house I saw Freddie closing the trunk of his car parked out front. Maddie and Lara were coming down the front walk.

"Where's Shelly?" I asked.

"One of her friend's parents died and she went to be with them. But we'll all fit in my car now," Freddie said. "It will save on gas because we don't have to take dad's SUV."

When we had packed into the car and started on the road, Freddie driving, Maddie asked me, "So how do you like it here so far?"

"Well enough," I answered and I told them about a few of my experiences of the week. They all knew the Czernaks and Maddie told me Janet was famous for inviting young people over. Then she asked me about the book of Revelations. She said she had just read it and was trying to learn about the signs of the end of the world. I told her I liked to read Exodus also for that because it teaches us about the wicked tricks of the enemy of souls in our day.

"For example," I said, "In Exodus 8, Pharaoh, who is a picture of the kingdom of this world and the ruler of the kingdom of this world, says, 'Entreat for me.' That is, 'Pray for me.' So this shows us one of the devil's ways of deceiving many is by false religion."

"Boy, that's true," Freddie said. "There are so many good people out there, good churchgoing people. I have many friends and work companions also like that. I can see them saying 'pray for me' to me and to each other."

I agreed. "And it's a good thing to pray. But the religion of this world is an outward religion and it only takes part of God's Word to heart. Sometimes much of God's Word is taken to heart—which is why those false faiths can be so deceiving. For example, look how Pharaoh talks in chapter 9. He almost sounds like a Christian." I read it off my screen: "'I have sinned this time: the Lord is righteous, and I and my people are wicked.' See here how true this is. I think many people in our day make this same confession, that there is a God, and that they sin and are wicked, and that God is righteous. But the condition of Pharaoh's heart is revealed by his next words. He asks Moses to pray to God that there would be no more hail. He minds earthly things. So you can see that his entire religion is a show. He doesn't care about getting to the promised land. What he really cares about is escaping punishment but still being able to sin and have things go well for him on this earth."

Maddie and Lara had been silent in the back seat for a while. Now Lara spoke. "I think it's good to read the Bible so that we are better able to understand how our world is, and how the devil operates."

Maddie agreed. "Yes, because sometimes things seem different from what the Bible describes. But if you read the Bible and go by what it says you can just believe that things are how they are, and not how they seem."

I had been looking on further in the text. "Yes," I said. "Look how in chapter 10—well, let me read it, here is what Pharaoh says to try to get out of punishment and have things go smoothly for him in this life only: 'Now therefore forgive, I pray thee, my sin only this once, and entreat the Lord your God, that he may take away from me this death only.'"

Maddie nodded. "Yes, I can see that he is just trying to partially confess, to get out of a situation that he does not like. He seems to agree with part of God's Word, when pressed, but one wonders why he says 'this once' and 'just this death only.' He sounds like Saul in chapter 15 of the first book of Samuel, who confesses some sin, but keeps back other sin."

"I think it's a good picture of the religions of this world—partial religions—they take part of the Word of God, and tread the rest underfoot, ignoring it," Freddie said.

We agreed with him and I wondered if I should bring up the Wednesday night meeting and get their take on it. But I decided against it, and we began to talk about the springtime and planting gardens and trips that we might plan for the summer.

It didn't seem like two and a half hours but that's how long it was before we were at Aunt Ella's. She let us into her little house, coming to the door in a walker. We heard the voice of a sermon in the living room and when we got there we saw she had put her ipad playing a sermon from the internet. We sat down and joined her in listening after quietly greeting and hugging her.

We sang for a while after the sermon, visited Aunt Ella, cleaned up her house a bit, helping her with things she could not do. When she napped we went for a walk and then came back and made dinner.

Aunt Ella was so grateful for us coming it made the trip worth it, even the long drive home, which passed quickly with more conversation and discussion. Even Lara opened up and I felt like I got to know her a little bit better.

When we got back to the Bonn's house, Shelly still wasn't home so I visited an hour with her folks and whoever was still up and then drove home.

I was home by eleven and so I read through my Sunday School lesson for the next day quickly and watered my plants and turned in. It had been a good day. I prayed to God as I fell asleep: "O God, save me from all those who persecute me, and deliver me, lest he tear my soul like a lion, rending it in pieces, while there is none to deliver . . ."

Chapter Twelve

I GOT UP EARLY ON Sunday morning, at seven. I had just set my first pot of coffee brewing when I heard my phone buzz. It was 7:03 am. The text was from Micah:

"Are you busy?"

Me:

"No, what's up?"

Micah:

"Are you worried that Mortin might be too strident?"

Me:

"Why don't you come over and visit?"

Micah:

"Sure, I'll be over there in ten."

Micah wouldn't look me in the eye for the first few minutes after he got to my house. We were standing in my kitchen. His dress shoes sat where Rachelle's heels had sat next to my slippers so recently.

"Whose lipstick is this?" Micah asked me.

"What?" He held a tube of bright red lipstick in his hand and was opening and closing the cover of it curiously.

"Oh. It must be Rachelle's. She was over the other night and we were in this kitchen. She must have set it on that bookshelf and then forgot about it."

"Heidi's sister? The one who looks like a model?"

"That's Rachelle."

"She came over?"

"To visit."

"Why are you blushing?"

"I'm not blushing," I said. "And, no, I don't think Mortin is too strident. We all have our stumblings, questions, concerns."

"So you don't want to have a meeting to discuss him."

"Definitely not. I don't even like this meeting you and I are having right now discussing the contents of someone else's heart, which no one can know."

"Is that what we're doing?"

"We're coming perilously close."

"Oh." Micah sat down. "So what do we do?"

"Watch and pray, that ye enter not into temptation. Just pray and let it go at that. And every time you see Mortin, be nice, and go out of your way to invite him over, and discuss things with him freely over coffee, openly and equally."

"I'll think about it," Micah said. And then he set his coffee down. We went out into the back and I absently pulled a few weeds out of some flowerpots next to the swing I was sitting on. Micah seemed like he wanted to say more, but instead he finally said, "I like your tomatoes. They're starting to look really good. Let me have some when they're ripe, okay?"

"Sure," I said. "I've got to get ready for church. Remember somewhere in Luke Jesus tells about a gardener. Others want to take down an unfruitful vine."

"Yes," Micah said.

"Jesus says, dig it and dung it and let it grow another year."

Chapter Thirteen

————◄○►————

WHEN I GOT TO the church I was early. All the Sunday School students and teachers were gathering in the sanctuary. I found my place, and just as I spotted Shelly sitting up front with the preschoolers and was about to go visit with her, I felt a tap on my shoulder. It was Erik. "Mortin is sick," he said. "He can't serve this morning. Can you serve?"

My heart began to beat faster. "Okay."

Since I was new, I didn't have to give the lesson to the eighth graders. Donald taught them and I watched his lesson and how he answered the students' questions at the end. I was glad because I had the chance to peruse the gospel text for the Sunday. It was a beautiful text but it didn't say anything to my mind this morning. I flipped through the pages of my Bible. I pulled out old Mr. Czernak's notebook. Nothing. I picked the garden dirt from under my fingernails. Then I set down my file and picked up my Bible again. The eighth graders were ignoring me for the most part. Not many of them knew me, and to them I'm sure I seemed old.

"And so Joshua warned about serving false gods, like their grandparents and others long ago had done far away in Babylon—what are some idols today?" Donald asked. But nobody could answer because the class time had run out so we all got up and made our way towards the sanctuary for the closing song gathering.

When the last hymn of the Sunday School was over I went straight into the sacristy. It was empty. I sat down before my Bible.

"Who is a God like unto thee," I read from Micah, "That pardoneth iniquity and passeth by the transgression of the remnant of his heritage? He retaineth not his anger forever, because he delighteth in mercy. He will turn again, he will have compassion on us; he will subdue our inquities . . ."

It was such a wonderful text, but as I read it my eyes kept going back to the first line: "Who is a God like thee?" And so I kept searching for a text.

The door opened. It was Donald. "Where have you been? The hymn has been sung. The congregation is waiting for you!"

I looked at the time. "Oh, no. I can't believe it's already time to speak. I'm on my way." I shut my Bible, turned off my phone, and walked out of the sacristy and up to the pulpit. I sat down, opened the Bible, and read: "And Simon answering said unto him, Master, we have toiled all the night, and have taken nothing: nevertheless at thy word I will let down the net. And when they had this done, they enclosed a great multitude of fishes: and their net brake. And they beckoned unto their partners, which were in the other ship, that they should come and help them. And they came, and filled both the ships, so that they began to sink. When Simon Peter saw it, he fell down at Jesus' knees, saying, Depart from me; for I am a sinful man, O Lord."